Having spent 22 years as a lorry driver, Julian was forced to retire due to ill health. So after looking around for something to occupy his time, he fell into the world of writing. One of the things Julian enjoys about writing children's books is how his imagination can take him into a different world, away from this one. The joy of watching a story appear in front of him and the delight and laughter Julian has from writing makes him wish that he started many years earlier. Having shown some of his stories to others and with encouragement, Julian now wants to share his stories with the children around the world.

Julian Edwards

Drip & Drop

The Water Gargoyles

AUSTIN MACAULEY PUBLISHERS™
LONDON • CAMBRIDGE • NEW YORK • SHARJAH

A CIP catalogue record for this title is available from the British Library.

ISBN 9781528932622 (Paperback)
ISBN 9781528932639 (Hardback)
ISBN 9781528942508 (ePub e-book)

www.austinmacauley.com

First Published (2021)
Austin Macauley Publishers Ltd
25 Canada Square
Canary Wharf
London
E14 5LQ

To my mum, Brian, Sylvia and Maureen for their help and encouragement in helping me start out as an author.

A special thank you to Caitlyn Simpson for her help in choosing the baby doe's name. I would also like to thank Robert Hooper for his amazing artwork for the book.

A stream flows lazily through the fields, until eventually it comes to a waterfall, where it falls, splashing into the lake, and sometimes, if the sun shines on it from a certain direction, a rainbow forms.

At the other end of the lake is the beginning of another stream that winds its way across the country, meeting canals and other streams and rivers, until it comes to the sea.

Due to the two streams, the water is crystal clear in the lake, and because of this, life thrives, with fishes, tadpoles and frogs, as well as plants, such as water lilies and reeds.

Otters live in the embankment, slipping in and out of the lake, all day long, using their webbed feet and strong tail to swim, as well as play with their family members.

Dragons and damselflies hover and fly above the lake as well, each one a different colour, such as blue, red and green, under a clear blue sky on a warm summer's day.

Yes, life thrives in full, around and in the lake, as well as in the trees and grass. It really is a sight to see. If you have time to go there and sit and watch, you will see nature put on a display.

In the middle of the lake there is an island, not a big island, but big enough for our friends, the water gargoyles, who I will tell you about very shortly; but first, I want to tell you about the tree.

The tree is an oak tree that has grown big and strong, with a very wide trunk and strong branches. The tree is covered with a crown of deep green leaves, especially in the months of summer.

The leaves not only make the oak tree look majestic,

but they also make a good hiding place for the little water gargoyles, as well as nesting for the birds so they can have their young.
But this oak tree is hiding a secret, which you must keep to yourself and promise not to tell anyone else, which I'm pretty sure you will, so here we go.
Where the branches grow from the tree, there are little doors, and these doors are used by the water gargoyles to peek outside to see if there is anything or anyone around.
But it is what is inside that makes things really interesting—oh yes it does. Behind each door, there is a landing platform, wide and strong enough for the water gargoyles to land on, as they have wings.
And inside the tree itself, it has been hollowed out, and it is here we will see a hive of activities, such as carpenters making furniture, as well as mending the broken ones too. As well as friends visiting each other to catch up on the news of the day, sharing the gossip and telling stories to the little water gargoyles who are still learning of time gone by past.
Over time, the walls inside the tree have been worn smooth from the water gargoyles leaning and rubbing against it, and it also smells like vanilla ice cream in there.
All year round, the inside is cool and fresh in the summer, and warm and comfortable in the depth of the harsh winter, keeping the water gargoyles safe from our old friend, Jack Frost.
At the bottom of the tree is an opening that leads to the homes of the water gargoyles that they have built inside the island itself, each one with its own little front door, made from the oak tree.

Behind each door, you will enter a passageway that has oak beams supporting the ceiling. On either side of the passageway is a little bedroom with a bed and side table that has a candle in its holder to chase away the gloom.

Further along the passage you will find another door, and behind it, you will see a little storage area for the things that the water gargoyles have found, in and around the lake, and decided to take home. Things, such as balls and little toy boats and bits of wood and stone, that to the water gargoyles are of interest and something to show and talk about with their friends and family.

And now, you finally come to the last room in the home of the water gargoyles, a round circular room with chairs and a table, so that they can have their friends around to visit.

It is here I will now introduce you to two particular water gargoyles that this story is about. One is called Drip and the other is called Drop, and these two patrol the lake–inside and outside–looking out for danger.

Drip and Drop have hands and feet like you and me, except, in between their fingers and toes, they have skin growing, and it's because of these skins they can swim very fast indeed.

On their necks, they have little gills that help them breath underwater, and their bodies have little silver scales, from head to toe, that sparkle in the sunshine and are very hard to see.

On their backs are two fins that are very special too, as they can unfold them and turn them in to wings, and because of these wings, they can fly high up in to the air and in to the trees.

All over, they are silver-grey in colour, including their faces, and they have a mouth each, as well as eyes and nose–just like you and me–and their ears are like little holes that are covered with a thin layer of skin to stop the water going in.

Drip and Drop are brothers, and like brothers, they look out for each other; although in Drip's case, Drop finds himself having to keep a closer eye on him because Drip does lives up to his namesake sometimes.

The two brothers live in the island–the one that I have already mentioned earlier–and to get to their home, they have to swim underneath the island to get to a tunnel that leads inside and to the tree.

Drip and Drop, like the other water gargoyles, spend their days swimming around the lake, as it is their job to report any changes to the king and queen of the lake, as well as to report any incoming danger to the other water gargoyles. They also have to keep watch on the surrounding trees and the wild animals that live there but the problem with Drip and Drop is that they do get very bored and start to play instead.

The sun, like all summer days, has been shining very bright today and was very hot indeed. So hot that the water of the lake has become very warm, indeed.

"Drip," said Drop to his brother. "I don't really fancy going home tonight, so how do you feel about sleeping in the old nest up in the oak tree instead?"

"OK," replied Drip, in response to his brother. "But it might rain though."

"Well does it really matter if it does rain?" asked Drop.

"Well, of course it does," replied Drip, to what he thought was a very silly question. "It would mean we would both get wet."
"Drip," said Drop kindly. "Unless you haven't noticed by now, we live and work in a lake, so that means we are always wet."
"That's a very good point, Drop," said Drip. "But can I ask you a question?"
"By all means," replied Drop, feeling very proud of himself.
"Do you go to bed whilst wet, at home?" asked Drip with a little twinkle in his eye.
"Well, of course I don't," replied Drop, laughing at Drip.
"So, why should sleeping in the nest be any different from sleeping inside then?" asked Drip, looking at Drop, who started to feel a bit of a drip.
"Ah," replied Drop, who suddenly felt like a drip. "That's a very good point."
"Exactly," said Drip, who was grinning from ear to ear and beginning to laugh at his brother.
"Oh, do shut up," said Drop kindly whilst laughing. "Come on, let's go and find the old nest."
With that, Drip and Drop shot towards the surface of the lake, their little legs moving up and down in a blur and as they swam, their wings started to unfold, ready for them to start flying once they were in the air. Whoosh!
"Did you know, dear reader, fishes have three problems in life?" said poor Mr Salmon as he swam unsteadily back to the safety of his home. "One is the fisherman, two is pollution, and three is them water gargoyles."
In the meantime, Drip and Drop soared up into the

air, leaving a trail of water behind them, up into the trees, and started to enjoy the warm summer evening breeze as it dried them off until they spied a nest.
"That will do?" said Drop, pointing to the nest in question.
"Oh, I don't know, Drop," said Drip, who was having doubts about it. "It looks as if it has been built recently."
"I don't really care," said Drop grumpily. "It has been a long day and all I want to do is lie down and go to sleep."
"Well, don't say I didn't warn you," said Drip, feeling a little bit worried.
"I won't," said Drop, still being grumpy. "I will promise you that if it makes you feel better."
"Well, OK then," said Drip, shrugging off his discomfort.
After getting a leaf each, to use to cover themselves up with, Drip and Drop laid down in the nest, until finally, as the sky darkened and the stars appeared shining in the night sky, Drip and Drop fell fast asleep.
Splash!
"What was that?" exclaimed Drip as he sat up suddenly.
After realising he wasn't going to get a response from Drop, who was still sleeping undisturbed, Drip decided to curl up again under his leaf and go back to sleep.
Splash!
"I definitely heard something this time," Drip muttered to himself worryingly.
With that, Drip decides to wake Drop up and tell

him what he had heard. So with a few shakes and finally a kick, Drip manages to wake Drop up.
"OW," yelled Drop. "What did you kick me for?" asked Drop crossly whilst rubbing his leg.
"Sorry about that, Drop," said Drip, who didn't mean to hurt Drop. "I was trying to wake you up."
"Well, I'm awake now," said Drop, more calmly. "So you better tell what is worrying you," Drop inquired, noticing Drip looked very worried.
So, Drip then proceeded to tell Drop that he had heard a splashing noise and that it woke him up twice in the night.
"Have you heard anything since?" asked Drop whilst thinking Drip must have been dreaming.
"No, I haven't," replied Drip, who was listening for any more noises.
"Well, it might be possible that you was dreaming," said Drop, not really caring as he wanted to go back to sleep.
"Do you think so?" said Drip, who was pretty sure he wasn't dreaming.
"I'm sure of it," said Drop, silently praying that Drip would settle back down.
"Well, alright then," said Drip, not entirely convinced.
"Come on," said Drop kindly. "Lie back down and try and get some more sleep as we have another long day tomorrow."
"Well, OK," said Drip, laying back down in the nest, until finally he fell asleep, with Drop watching over him.
"Chirp, chirp, chirp," sang Mr Robin, looking at Drip and Drop as they lay fast asleep whilst the sun started to rise to begin a new day.
"CHIRP, CHIRP," Mr Robin sang louder whilst Drip

and Drop still slept on soundly.
Wow, thought Mr Robin. These two really don't want to wake up at all today, lazy little monkeys.
Mr Robin then decided to hop into the nest and then started to nudge Drip and Drop with his little talons, until he finally succeeded in waking them.
"Drip, pack it in, will you? I'm tired, still," said Drop, rather crossly, upon waking up.
"It's not me," said poor Drip defensively. "It was Mr Robin who is to blame." Drip turned to point at Mr Robin.
"Oh, hello, Mr Robin. Are you OK?" said Drop, noticing Mr Robin for the first time after awaking.
"I will be when you two get up because I will start pecking at you both," said Mr Robin, rather more crossly than he meant to.
"OK, OK," said Drip and Drop together whilst getting up from the floor of the nest.
"Are you OK, Mr Robin?" asked Drip, whilst Drop started to have a stretch. "You are not your normal cheerful self today, which is very unusual for you."
"Well, I've hardly had any sleep last night," said Mr Robin, who was starting to feel guilty for snapping at Drip and Drop.
"Well I've had a lovely night sleep," said Drop, not paying much attention to Mr Robin.
"I can see that," said Mr Robin, cocking his head to one side and starting to get even more annoyed.
"What happened?" said Drip calmly to Mr Robin, as he could see that Mr Robin was getting angry. "Tell me all about it, please."
"Hedge gargoyles are what happened," said Mr Robin, whilst pacing round the nest floor. "All night long they did nothing but moan and whine,

without stopping."
"I wonder who that reminds me of?" whispered Drop to Drip, with a quite chuckle.
"Oh dear," said Drip, whilst trying not to laugh at Drop's remark. "What has started them off this time, Mr Robin?"
"Well," said Mr Robin, "during the night, a two-legged came walking by and decided to push something into the hedge, and the noise is what woke up the hedge gargoyles."
"Couldn't they have left it until the morning?" asked Drop, whilst thinking he might have just asked a silly question, for some reason.
"I take it you haven't met hedge gargoyles before, Drop?" replied Mr Robin, in response to Drop's question.
"No, I haven't. But I have heard of them," replied Drop. Then turning to Drip, he said, "Have you met any hedge gargoyles, Drip?"
"No, I haven't met any," replied Drip. "But I wouldn't mind doing so."
"I see," said Mr Robin, looking at Drip and Drop. "It looks like I'm going to have to tell you both about the hedge gargoyles."
"If you wouldn't mind," said Drop, who really would like to learn more about the hedge gargoyles.
"Yes, please tell us, Mr Robin," said Drip, who was suddenly very curious. "That way we will know what to expect if we should ever meet any."
"Hedge gargoyles are angry little creatures," said Mr Robin as he started his explanation. "And for good reasons really, as they always seem to be the ones who keep getting disturbed by the two legs. The reason for that is because hedgerows are

found in fields or gardens, and are easier for a two legs to push their rubbish into, rather than put their rubbish in a bin."

"Oh my," said Drop, who was shocked from Mr Robin's explanation. "How horrible for them...no wonder they are grumpy."

"Can I ask what it was that was pushed into the hedge?" said Drip, who, like Drop, didn't like what he was hearing.

"I've no idea what it was," said Mr Robin, replying to Drip.

"Could you describe it, do you think?" asked Drop.

"I will certainly try," replied Mr Robin. "It is round in shape, and it was red like my red chest, and the top and bottom of it is like shiny silver."

"It doesn't ring any bells to me," said Drop. Then turning to Drip, he said, "Do you have any idea, Drip?"

"Nothing is coming to my mind," said Drip, shaking his head. Then he added, "What I don't understand is why didn't they push it back out of the hedge?"

"Two reasons," replied Mr Robin. "One, the hedge gargoyles are very small creatures, smaller than you two; and two, when I suggested the idea to them, they became very cross with me."

"I can't see why they should be cross with you, Mr Robin, as it seems to me like a very reasonable suggestion," said Drip whilst Drop was looking at him in amazement, as he had never really known his brother to use too many long words, especially two together in a sentence.

"The problem with the hedge gargoyles, Drip, is that they really can't stand things being untidy," said Mr Robin, who was wishing he be allowed to forget the previous night.

"I can see their point, really," said Drop, looking at the clean, crystal-clear water of the lake below him, from his standing point on the tree branch, and suddenly feeling very proud of his home.

"Well, I don't know. I'm not sure," said Drip, throwing his arms up into the air. Then he said, "Anyway, enough of that now, Mr Robin. Why don't you rest here, and try and catch up on your sleep."

"Good idea, Drip," said Drop, agreeing with his brother. "We have to get back now anyway, as I'm pretty sure we will be late if we are not careful."

"Well, thank you both for your kindness," said Mr Robin. "Not that I deserve your kindness with being so cross with you both for no reasons, and for that I'm very sorry, indeed."

"Oh, that's alright, Mr Robin," said Drip and Drop, together.

"You just rest now and don't let it bother you another moment longer," said Drip, feeling sorry for poor Mr Robin.

"I agree with Drip on that," said Drop to Mr Robin. "But we really must be going now, so I will say goodbye to you."

"Goodbye, boys," said Mr Robin. "And thank you again for your forgiveness."

"Goodbye, Mr Robin," said Drip, waving to Mr Robin.

As Mr Robin settled down to get some well-earned sleep, Drip and Drop turned and started to run along the branch of the tree they were in, and then when they came to the end, they dived down towards the lake.

And it is here they will learn how important it is to always look before they jumped, a lesson they will

never forget.
"Look out, you two," screeched the voice of Mrs Owl who was flying below them. "BELOW THE WATER, LOOK OUT," Mrs Owl then screeched even louder.
On seeing the objects below the surface of the lake, Drip and Drop extended their wings to change their dive into flight and just managed to skim along the surface of the lake, missing the objects by inches.
Because of the rush from the dive and fright, Drip and Drop didn't really have control of their flight which meant that they both ended up crashing into the embankment.
"What were those things?" asked Drip, after a short while, to his brother whilst trying to catch his breath from the fright he was suffering from as he laid spread eagle on the ground.
"I don't know, Drip," replied Drop whilst trying to stand up. "But we need to go and have a proper look. But before we do, I need to get my breath back." With that, Drop then collapsed back onto the ground, to lie down next to Drip.
"Are you both OK?" said Mrs Owl, who in the meantime had landed on a fallen tree trunk near Drip and Drop. "That looked like a bad accident from where I was," Mrs Owl then added.
"We are fine, thank you, Mrs Owl," said Drop. Then looking at Drip, he said, "Are you OK, Drip?"
"Yes, I'm OK," replied Drip, who was more interested in looking at the blue sky above him from where he laid on the ground.
"Are you both sure?" asked Mrs Owl, not quite ready to believe Drip and Drop. "Because it looked like you both landed quite hard, you know."
"We're fine, honestly, Mrs Owl, please don't worry,"

said Drip, from the ground, and was starting to feel little twinges of pain all over his body.

"Well, that's good to hear," said Mrs Owl. She then went on to say, rather crossly, I might add, "Do you pair realise how silly you have both been? Not only did you both nearly hit me, you both nearly killed yourselves. Honestly, I've never seen such silliness in all my days."

Silence descended on the embankment. Drip and Drop did not dare to move or speak for fear of being told off again by Mrs Owl and weren't quite sure if they were allowed to speak or if it would be best to remain quiet.

"Well," said Mrs Owl sternly and still feeling cross, "do you both have anything to say or has something got your tongue?"

"Mrs Owl," said Drop, slowly and carefully, as he thought about what he was going to say next, "I and Drip are very sorry, and you are quite right about us both being silly, and yes, we should have looked before we jump."

"I'm very sorry too, Mrs Owl," said Drip, wishing the ground would swallow him. "We were very silly, indeed, and we will promise not to do it again."

"Very well, then," said Mrs Owl. Then in a calmer voice, she added, "I only got cross with you two because I've known you both since you were children, and I love and care about you, and I don't want to lose you both. Now come and give me a cuddle, you silly pair."

Drip and Drop got to their feet and flew over to Mrs Owl who opened up her wings to wrap around them, and there, just for a few moments, stood Mrs Owl and Drip and Drop, cuddling each other.

Afterwards, with a goodbye from everyone, Mrs Owl took to the air to carry on flying home but not before circling overhead to have one last look at Drip and Drop, before disappearing into the distance.
After a short while, Drip and Drop slid into the crystal-clear water of the lake from the embankment, and then, with a little more care and caution, swam over towards the two very strange looking items that lay at the bottom of the lake.
"These must have been thrown in last night," said Drip to Drop, after looking at the items for a moment. "And that is what woke me up too. Which also means I wasn't dreaming after all?"
"You are right, Drip," said Drop, looking at his brother. "In future, if you are woken up again from a noise, we must go and investigate."
"OK," said Drip, patting Drop on his shoulder. "Come on, we better go and take a closer look."
Drip and Drop then swam even closer to the items in question. "Look, one of these items has two big round things on it, and the other one has four little round things on it as well," Drip said, pointing to each item. "I think these must be wheels."
"I think you are right, Drip," said Drop, swimming even closer. "But what is that shiny round thing over there, I wonder?"
"What round shiny thing?" asked Drip, looking hard for the item Drop mentioned but failing to see it. "I can't see what you are talking about."
"Over here," said Drop, pointing to the round shiny thing.
"I see it now," said Drip. "Come on, let's have a closer look at it."

"Well, I don't know if that would be a good idea, Drip," said Drop, backing away whilst looking at the item with suspicion.
"Well, let's look at it this way, Drop," said Drip. "Do you want to be the one to tell the king and queen that we have found these items but don't know anything about them because we weren't brave enough to investigate? Because I certainly don't."
"Well, since you put it like that, then no, I don't," replied Drop, feeling a little bit put out. "But before we go, I need to ask you something that has been bothering me."
"What is that?" asked Drip, feeling a little bit worried all of a sudden.
"Are you feeling alright?" asked Drop. "Because you seem to be behaving differently than normal."
"Yes, I'm feeling fine," replied Drip, looking at Drop with suspicion. "Why, don't I look fine?"
"Yes, you look very well," answered Drop, backing away from Drip.
"Well, what is the problem then?" asked Drip, who was starting to feel a little bit put out.
"Well, I've noticed you have been using a lot of long words lately, which isn't normal for you," said Drop, who for some strange reasons felt he needed to be ready to run.
"Drop," said Drip, trying not to be cross. "I often use long words and have done so for many years. So it might help you if you were to pay more attention to what I'm saying in future."
"You are right, Drip," said Drop, feeling very foolish indeed. He then said, "I'm very sorry for not paying more attention to what you are saying, and while I'm thinking about it, I'm going to apologize for not

believing you last night as well."

"Right," said Drip. "Thank you for your apologies. Now, can we please go and look at that shiny thing, and then we will have to go and report to the king and queen before long or we will be in trouble."

"OK, OK," said Drop, chuckling. "Calm down, we have plenty of time."

As Drip and Drop swam over to the round shiny thing, they noticed, as they got closer, a little lever sticking out from the side of it.

"I wonder if it moves," said Drip, taking hold of it with both hands.

"See if you can move it," said Drop, who had decided he wasn't going anywhere near it just yet. "But please be careful."

Drip took a firm hold of the lever and tried to move it, even trying to move it whilst upside down, but after struggling with it for a few minutes, Drip said, "I can't move it, Drop. You are going to have to help me, I'm afraid."

Drop, seeing that it was safe, swam over to his brother and then, with both of them taking a firm grip of the little lever, they pulled as hard as they could, when suddenly it moved, and as it did so, it made a glug-glug-glug noise. Drip and Drop both shot backwards whilst both exclaiming, "Whoa," in surprise and fright, that they ended up getting slightly entangled in the reeds that grew behind them on the bottom of the lake.

After getting their breath back, for the second time that day, and looking at the shiny thing in awe, Drip said, "Wow, let's do that again. I want to hear that strange noise again."

So after untangling themselves from the reeds,

Drip and Drop swam back to the little round shiny thing, to start moving the little lever backwards and forwards again whilst laughing at the strange glug-glug noise that came from it. Whilst Drip and Drop were busy pulling the lever and making more glug-glug noises, they didn't notice that two female water gargoyles had swum over and were busy watching them.

Plip and Plop looked exactly the same as Drip and Drop, except for their long silvery hair that had been left to grow down the full length of their backs, and because of this, their hair swayed with the movement of the current in the lake.

It's only the lady water gargoyles that have long silver hair, except for the queen, whose hair is golden that glitters and sparkles when she is out flying in the sunshine, which the queen often does.

Because Drip and Drop weren't paying attention whilst still busy playing instead, they both ended up getting entangled in the reeds again from the fright and surprise of hearing Plop say, "Hello, you two, what are you up to?"

Drop looked for his brother but did not succeed in finding Drip whilst still tangled in the reeds, and said, "Is it me or are we both having a fright day here?"

"I don't know, Drop," groaned Drip from somewhere behind Drop, "but it would be nice if it would please stop, as I really don't think I can take any more of this."

"Are you both OK?" said Plip, who, in the meantime, had swam over to where Drip and Drop were, closely followed by Plop.

"Hi Plip, hi Plop, we were just exploring those

strange things," said Drop, who was in the process of getting back to his feet.
"Hello ladies," said Drip, who was struggling to untangle himself from the reeds, until Plip swam over to help him, and then finally everyone was together.
"I see," said Plop, not believing a word Drop had said. "Don't you actually really mean to say you were busy playing?"
"Might be," said Drop, feeling embarrassed all of the sudden.
"Have you told the king and queen yet?" asked Plop, looking at both Drip and Drop.
"No we haven't. Not yet," replied Drop, trying to regain some sort of control on the situation.
"Well, don't you think you should have done so by now?" asked Plop sternly.
"We have only just got here ourselves, Plop," replied Drop defensively.
"Huh, a likely story, I'm sure," said Plop grumpily.
"Wow," said Drip as he and Plip moved away from the other two. "Is your sister always like this, or is she just having a bad day?"
"She is not always like this," replied Plip. "But when she is, I find it is best to keep out of the way, just in case she starts on me."
"Do you know why she is like it today?" asked Drip, looking at Plop.
"I think it's because she is tired," replied Plip, who was feeling a little bit embarrassed for her sister. "She didn't sleep very well last night."
"Do you mind if I stay with you?" asked Drip, looking at Plip. "For safety reasons," Drip then added, causing Plip to laugh.

"Of course you can, Drip," replied Plip. "It is nice to have some company as well," Plip then added as she did quite like being with Drip.

So for the moment, we will leave Drip and Plip and return to Drop and Plop who were coming to the end of their discussion, or more to the point what Plop was saying and poor Drop had to listen, whether he liked it or not.

"Right," said Plop, still being grumpy towards Drop. "Me and Plip will go and inform the king and queen whilst you two carry on playing."

"OK, OK," said Drop. He thought to himself, I really wish you would go away, Plop, although not unkindly.

"Come on, Plip, we're going to the palace," Plop turned as she called out to her sister.

"OK," replied Plip to her sister and then she turned to follow Plop to the palace of the king and queen but not before giving Drip a kiss on his cheek, leaving him to float in the water.

"You know something, Drip," said Drop, who hadn't seen what Plip had done to Drip. "Plop really can be so annoying at times. I will even go as far as to say she can even be impossible at times, too." He watched as the sisters departed.

"She is really lovely, isn't she?" said Drip, who wasn't really paying attention to anything Drop was saying, as he was in a world of his own at that moment.

"What?" exclaimed Drop, turning to face his brother, only to be faced with a surprise. "Drip," Drop then said more kindly. "Why are you upside down?"

"My world has been turned upside down," replied Drip, who really was by now in a state of bliss.

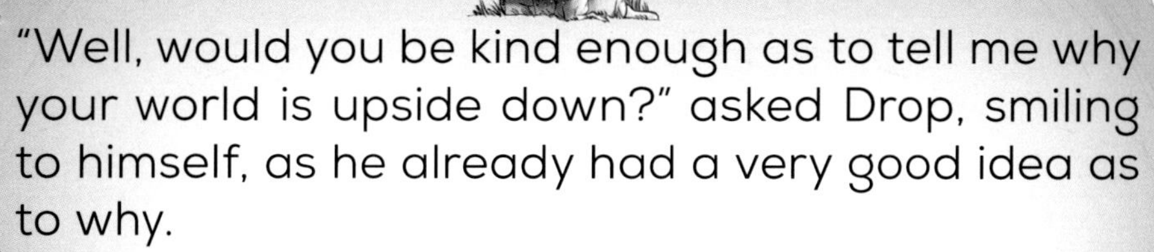

"Well, would you be kind enough as to tell me why your world is upside down?" asked Drop, smiling to himself, as he already had a very good idea as to why.

"Plip kissed me on the cheek," replied Drip, who now felt like he had butterflies in his belly.

"Oh, for goodness sake, Drip, it was only a kiss," said Drop, chuckling to himself.

"I know it was," said Drip, dreamily. "But it felt so much more than that."

Oh dear, thought Drop to himself whilst shaking his head and looking up at the sun shining through the lake surface from his position on the bottom of the lake.

"I know!" exclaimed Drip, suddenly turning the right way up and feeling a little bit dizzy for it. "Why don't we all go out together one day?"

"What do you mean, Drip?" asked Drop, who already had a pretty good idea what Drip meant but wanted him confirming.

"Me and Plip, and you and Plop will all go out together one day," replied Drip, whose mind was already filled with showing Plip the surrounding trees that grew by the lake.

"Oh, no, no, no," said Drop, who just knew what was coming. "Absolutely not. Thank you very much."

"Well, why not?" asked Drip, who was secretly hoping for Drop's support. "It could be fun you know."

"Fun," said Drop. "Have you seen how Plop behaved today? I don't even think Plop knows how to have fun, as she is far too serious to even know what fun is. Anyways, I'm happy as I am, thank you very much."

"And what way is that exactly?" asked Drip, not really believing what Drop had just said.
"Being single," replied Drop, who actually liked Drip's idea now that he thought about it a little bit, not that he was going to admit to it though.
"Well, alright then. If that's how you feel," said Drip whilst shrugging his shoulders in defeat. "I'm pretty sure I will think of something else before long."
After a few seconds had gone by, Drip then said, "I've just had a thought, Drop."
"Does this thought involve Plop?" asked Drop, looking at Drip suspiciously.
"No, it doesn't," replied Drip with a wry chuckle.
"Oh, good," said Drop, feeling himself filled with relief. "So, what is this thought of yours then?"
"Those objects must have been thrown in here by those two legs," replied Drip whilst looking at the objects in question. "Because if you remember from what Mr Robin was saying this morning, it seems to me that some of these two legs really don't care at all where they throw their rubbish."
"Must be true," said Drop whilst nodding his head slowly in agreement.
"Let's ask the king when he gets here," said Drip, "because I can see him coming now."
In the distance, Drip and Drop could see a golden glow moving steadily towards them. After a short while, the king of the water gargoyles arrived at the items in question, with Plip and Plop in tow, as well as two of his personal guards to inspect the objects.
The king was the same as Drip and Drop, except his whole body was covered in golden scales; scales that were so tiny that it was very difficult to see

them. He also had a little white beard that he played with when he was thinking about things. But before I carry on with the story, this is probably going to be the right time to tell you about the palace that is home to the king and queen of the water gargoyles. The palace has been built into the rocks that have been found, many years ago, by the water gargoyles behind the waterfall that falls, crashing into the lake, and it is here you will find two big gates that have been made from a big stone slab. The slab gates have been worn smooth over many long years by the waterfall. So smooth that when they are closed, it actually looks like a smooth rock face, and because of this, no one will ever know it was there.

Behind the gates, you will enter a long tunnel that has been built from the rock and has been smoothed down all the way to the other end, and on both sides are statues of kings and queens long gone.

The statues of the kings line the tunnel on the right-hand side and the queens are on the left-hand side. This way the kings and queens, who were together and married in life, can still look at each other for the rest of eternity.

In between each statue, stands a guard. Each one has silver scales, like Drip and Drop, except for the little glints of gold scales found on their arms, so that everyone will know that this particular water gargoyle is a royal guard. Each guard stands with their legs slightly apart and they also wear a blue cloak that is affixed to their neck and hangs down to the floor. They also have a wooden spear each, with a metal tip made from the oak tree, ready to

defend the palace.
At the other end of the tunnel, you will come to two big oak doors (I wonder where they came from) that open to reveal a grand room, where you will see two golden thrones, for the king and queen.
The doors have been built strong and sturdy with strong hinges to support and hold them firmly to the rock walls, and have been worked on until the wood is smoothed and polished.
Upon entering the grand throne room, you will see the walls are adorned with pictures of family members and friends of the king and queen. There are also tapestries of different colour, such as blue and gold, and on each different one are pictures of different animals.
Such as deer's and stag's, as well as pictures of castles and battle scenes that have happened, hundreds of years ago. Each one has been carefully woven together, so that they will last for many a long year.
But since the water gargoyles are not a fighting race any more, you wouldn't find any old swords or battle armour, since these have been destroyed, apart from the spears that the royal guards have that is part of their uniform. The water gargoyles prefer to use their magic instead to defend themselves. Magic that only the king and queen have and could use if they are sure no one will be harmed, including the two legs.
The two thrones, like the doors, are made from oak and are covered over with a thin layer of gold, making it appear as if they have been made out of gold. Each one has a blue cushion, with gold edgings, so that the king and queen can sit

in comfort.
After all sitting on a hard surface for a long while, like the king and queen do when receiving guests to the palace, can really start to hurt your bum after a while.
The king and queen are covered with golden scales, yet their faces are brown and weather worn with little wrinkles and gentle eyes, and you wouldn't be wrong if you saw kindness there.
Like Drip and Drop, they both have skin between each finger and toes, and golden wings on their backs. Whilst they are in the palace, they wear a cloak, like the guards, except theirs are golden instead of blue and have a crown over a waterfall woven into them.
The queen, like Plip and Plop, has hair that falls like a golden waterfall that sparkles in the sun, yet the king doesn't have any hair but does have a white-silvery beard that he has a habit of playing with.
Sometimes, especially in the summer months, the king and queen like to escape the palace and the guards to go up to the top of the oak tree to spend time on their own and reflect on their busy days.
They have their own little private place, among the leaves of the oak tree, where they can still keep an eye on the lake below and the surrounding area, but they mainly go there to sleep under the stars.
Now, it is time for us to return to the story of our water gargoyles, Drip and Drop.
"Mmm," said the king, looking at the objects lying on the lake floor. "I've seen these before, many years ago," the king then said, turning to the others.
"Can you recall what they are, your majesty?" asked Plop respectfully.

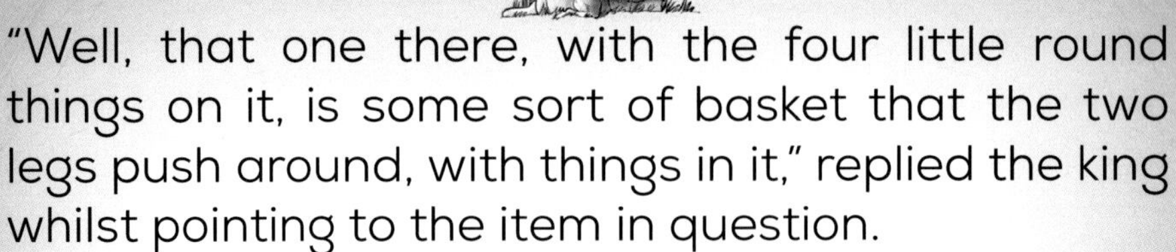

"Well, that one there, with the four little round things on it, is some sort of basket that the two legs push around, with things in it," replied the king whilst pointing to the item in question.
"What about the other one, your majesty?" asked Drop even more respectfully to try and annoy Plop.
"I would need to take a closer look at it, Drop," replied the king. "Whilst I'm doing so, why don't you two tell me what you have found out about these things so far?"
"We know that the shiny thing over there makes a glug, glug, glug noise," replied Drip, feeling proud of himself as he swam over to show the king the round shiny thing.
"Been having some fun, have we, boys?" The king chuckled, looking at Drip and Drop with a smile. "We better take closer look at those round things then, don't we?"
After swimming closer, they all noticed two other big round things affixed to a frame, and one of the round things had a smaller round thing attach to it on the side, as well as a bigger one attached to the bottom of the frame between the two big round things.
Now, I don't know about you but I'm certainly feeling a little bit dizzy talking about all these round things, whoa!
"Ahh, I see," said the king. "This one has teeth on it and it has something going round it that leads to another one that is smaller and is connected to this big round thing over here." He pointed to each item as he spoke. "So I'm assuming these arm things are connected to the big one with the teeth on it, and it is what makes it all go. Now if my memory is

serving me correctly, this is something that the two legs use to travel on."

"Wow," chorused Plop and Drop together, yet trying very hard to understand—as I am too—to what the king had just been explaining about at length, and decided to give up on it, as it sounded very complicated indeed.

"I can also tell you both that love is around us at the moment," said the king wisely, noticing something the others hadn't.

"Oh, I can assure you, your majesty, me and Drop are not together, sir," said Plop hurriedly and feeling embarrassed.

"Absolutely not," said Drop, agreeing with Plop, as well as feeling a little bit hot and bothered.

"I wasn't talking about you two at all," said the king. "I was talking about them two," he said, nodding in Drip and Plip's direction, who had both wandered off together and were now in a world of their own, holding each other's hands whilst looking into each other's eyes, as they drifted round in circles.

"Well, I—" Plop started to say angrily before she was interrupted very calmly by the king.

"Now, now, Plop," said the king, taking hold of Plop's hands gently and looking at her with his gentle eyes. "You know as well as I do that we can't interfere with what nature or fate intends for us, my dear."

"I'm sorry, your majesty. You are right as always," said Plop, hanging her head in shame for her anger and going red with embarrassment as well.

"There's no need to be sorry, my dear," said the king, gently, and releasing Plop's hands. "We all feel that we have to look after our family and close friends but we all need to know when to let go and walk

away too"
"It will be alright, Plop," said Drop with a smile and then taking Plop's hands into his own, he gave them a gentle squeeze, before releasing them again. "I know how you feel, so if you want to, we can both look after them if you like."
"I would like that very much, Drop," said Plop, looking at Drop. "Thank you for that and I'm sorry for being grumpy with you earlier."
"Very good," said the king whilst Drop was looking at Plop with renewed admiration. "It's surprising how a little bit of kindness goes a long way these days. In the meantime, you two will have to keep a watchful eye on things, as Drip and Plip seem to be in a world of their own to me.
"Don't worry, your majesty," said Drop, holding Plop's hand, much to her delight. "Me and Plop will sort things here."
"Excellent," said the king. "Right then, I better go and tell the queen what you have found out and try and explain what they are, which should be interesting. So, I will now say goodbye to you both and would be grateful if you could say goodbye to Drip and Plip for me as well please."
"We will do that for you, your majesty," said Plop, with Drop, nodding in agreement.
"Goodbye then, my dears," said the king. "Take care of yourselves and I will see you all again soon."
And with that, the king turned to swim away, followed closely by his two guards.
"Goodbye, your majesty," Drop and Plop called after him, with a wave, as he disappeared into the distance.
Then Plop turned to Drop. "What do you think we

should do now?" asked Plop, looking at Drop with excitement in her eyes.
"Right then," replied Drop whilst rubbing his hands together with glee. "As you know, the king said we need to keep an eye on things. And those things didn't just appear from inside the lake so that means a two legs must have thrown them in. So we will have to go up into the trees and see if we can see any two legs wandering around."
"Erm..." said Plop, looking a bit worried. "Me and Plip haven't been into the trees before Drop."
"Really!" exclaimed Drop, in shock and surprise.
"Yes, really," replied Plop defensively. "Plus it is safer down here in the lake, as me and Plip are not as brave as you and Drip either."
"Oh, Plop," said Drop kindly whilst squeezing Plop's hand in reassurance.
"You and Plip don't know what you have both been missing all this time."
"That maybe so," said Plop sulkily. "We can't help it if we are not as brave as you two."
"That may be true," said Drop kindly. "But I will promise you that you and Plip will be fine if you both stay close to me and Drip, until you both know your way round. Trust me."
"OK, I trust you, Drop," said Plop, smiling and feeling assured by Drop's words. "Shall we go and tell Drip and Plip now?"
"Yes," replied Drop, turning to look at Drip and Plip. "That's if we can pull them apart though."
After finally pulling Drip and Plip apart, Drop and Plop then proceeded to tell them what the king had said, as well as explain to them about the objects and what the king thought they were. Drop then

informed them of his idea of going up into the trees to keep a look out for any two legs who might be wandering around the area.

After reassuring Plip she would be quite safe as long as she stayed closed by, all four water gargoyles, whilst giving poor Mr Salmon another fright, shot up from the lake into the air and then flew over to the forest surrounding the lake. After flying around for a little while, they settled on a tree that had a wide view point overlooking the lake and the edge of the forest, and from there, they could see all around the lake's embankments.

"Wow," said Plop, looking around her in amazement at the view of the lake and the surrounding trees. "This is really amazing."

"This is so cool," said Plip, filling up with excitement, as well as feeling as free as a bird. "I really want to go and explore now."

"Oh no, you are not," said Plop rather sternly. "Not on your own, anyway."

"Plop," said Drop, taking hold of Plop's hand again and giving it a gentle squeeze. "She will be fine, so please try and calm down."

"She might get hurt or lost," said Plop, looking at Drop not preparing to give up that easily.

"Plop," said Plip, pulling Plop gentling round to face her. "I love you dearly and you know I do. But you need to let me grow in my own way now, and let me make my own mistakes. Otherwise, I'm not going to learn anything in life."

"I will go with her if you want me to?" said Drip, seeing how worried Plop is. "At least until she knows her way around the forest."

"Oh OK," said Plop, admitting defeat, and

remembering the king's wise words, as well as realising she isn't going to win anyway. "But, please, promise me you will be careful."
"I will, I promise you," said Plip with a squeal of delight. "Come on, Drip, what are you waiting for? Let's go."
"OK, OK, I'm coming," replied Drip whilst laughing at Plip's excitement.
Plip and Drip ran along the branch they were on, and then at the very last moment, they unfolded their wings and took off into the air, leaving Plop and Drop to watch after them until they disappeared into the distance.
"Right then," said Drop, settling back down against the tree trunk, with his legs stretched out, after watching Drip and Plip disappear. "Let's settle down now, Plop, and keep the watch, shall we?"
"Oh, alright," replied Plop sulkily, still looking after the disappearing Drip and Plip, who have, by now, flown out of sight.
So there, Plop and Drop sat high up in the tree keeping an eye on what is going on around the lake and the surrounding forest, and noticing that other water gargoyles were watching as well from the oak tree in the distance.
"Do you think they are alright, Drop?" Plop asked after a little while.
"Oh, I know they are alright," replied Drop, answering Plop's question with confidence.
"Well, how can you be so sure?" asked Plop, not quite sure whether to believe Drop or not, then deciding to trust him instead, like he asked her to.
"If you listen carefully, you will hear the occasional whoo-hoo noise," replied Drop, feeling quite

pleased with himself. "Look at them pair having fun whilst we are sitting up here doing our job."
"Oh yes," said Plop, listening carefully. "You are right, Drop. I wish we could go and have some fun as well though," Plop added, wishfully.
"Well, why don't we?" asked Drop, feeling exactly the same as Plop, as he was getting bored as well.
"Because someone got to be responsible around here," replied Plop, kicking her heels and getting fed up.
"Suit yourself," said Drop, leaning against the tree trunk and shutting his eyes.
Listening carefully, Drop could hear Plop moving around as she flew from branch to branch, as curiosity was starting to get the better of her, so much so, she was about to explode from it.
Mmmm, thought Drop to himself with a smile. Any moment now.
"Drop," said Plop, finally letting curiosity get the better of her, "I'm seriously bored now, so can we please go and join Plip and Drip in exploring the forest."
I just knew that was coming, thought Drop whilst laughing out loud.
"Drop," said Plop, pulling at Drop's feet and getting impatient. "Come on, will you."
"OK, OK," said Drop, getting to his feet and taking hold of Plop's hand tightly. "Let's go then, shall we?"
Off they both flew, zipping between branches and going round and round tree trunks until they were both dizzy and in fits of laughter, until eventually, they caught up with Drip and Plip.
All four of them were laughing, screaming and yelling with delight as they flew through the forest,

until a little incident happened that turned into a delight for everyone, including you, the reader, and it's here I will tell you all about it.
Plip, like the others, was flying through the forest, when she decided to look behind her, whilst in flight, only to see she was alone and had gotten herself lost. When she turned her head forward, she nearly hit a tree.
Plip swerved to miss the tree, but the shock and fright of what could have been made her lose control of her flying and this caused her to fall to the ground.
Plip screamed out loud and tried to regain control of her flight but sadly this wasn't to be, as Plip fell. She closed her eyes, until suddenly, everything stopped.
"Hello, my dear," said a gentle voice, sounding concerned. "Are you alright, there?"
"I think so," replied Plip, feeling no pain anywhere after her fall. "Where am I?" Plip then asked whilst looking around her, as well as looking for the owner of the gentle voice, only to find she is in a wide opening in the forest somewhere.
"You are lying on top of me," replied the voice, with a chuckle. "Luckily I saw you falling, otherwise you would have made me jump."
"Oh," said Plip, realising she could feel fur beneath her hands. "I do apologize for that. I hope you can forgive me, as I didn't mean to fall on top of you."
"Oh, there is nothing to apologize for," said the gentle voice, with another chuckle. "Why don't you climb down, if you feel OK to do so, and tell me your name? I can assure you, I mean you no harm."
Plip got to her feet, then stretched and checked her

wings to make sure that there is no damage and that she hasn't broken them in any way or form. Once she was happy, she then started moving them and then flew to the ground.

Upon landing, she then turned to look at the owner of the gentle voice, only to be faced with a giant of an animal, bearing in mind, water gargoyles are only six inches high.

No matter how hard she tried, Plip couldn't stop the overwhelming fear that washed through her and it didn't help matters when she saw a little head lift up and look at her from behind the owner of the gentle voice.

Meanwhile, Drip, Drop and Plop had realised that Plip had gone missing, and were now looking for her.

During the course of looking for Plip, Drip froze at the exact same moment Plip screamed as she fell, and so by using his senses, he called to the others to follow him.

"Where are we going, Drip?" asked Plop, who was frantic with worry and nearly in tears.

"This way," replied Drip, pointing into the forest as he flew. "I can sense her somewhere over there."

"Trust him, Plop," said Drop taking hold of Plop's hand whilst in flight. "If he says he can sense her, then be assured he can sense her."

After a short while, Drip came to a stop, hovering in mid-air, with Drop and Plop next to him. The reason for this was because, by now, Plip was knocked out, which is why Drip had lost all senses of her.

"What's happening, Drip?" asked Plop, not quite understanding what is going on. "What have we stopped here for?"

"I've lost her," replied Drip, sadly, who wasn't at all happy with the whole situation.
"Well, what is that supposed to mean?" cried out Plop, who was by now heartbroken and sick with worry.
"I don't know, Plop," replied Drip angrily and feeling guilty for being so. "I just don't know," he then said more calmly.
Drop took Plop into his arms and held her as she cried for the loss of her sister, Plip, until the tears stopped and the sobbing noise quietened down. It was here, Drop said to Plop quietly whilst still holding her, "I can't even begin to imagine what you are going through, Plop." Plop looked at him with tear-filled eyes. "But you need to trust Drip. I know it's hard." He held his hand up to stop Plop from saying anything. "But that brother of mine has something inside him that will help him find Plip."
"Shhh," hissed Drip, suddenly, because it was at that moment, he felt Plip filled with overwhelming fear. "This way, quickly now," Drip then said sharply.
As Plip stood there, frozen with fear, Drip came rushing through the air, going right up to the animal and yelling loudly, "LEAVE HER ALONE."
Whilst Drip was yelling, Drop bravely placed himself between Plip and the animal whilst Plop rushed to Plip's side, swooping Plip up into her arms and holding her tight. But then things took a surprising turn.
The giant animal lurched forward slightly, knocking the breath out of Drip and sending him to the forest floor, then said, in a gentle voice, "Drip, it's me, don't you recognise me at all?"
Drip looked up, as the other water gargoyles

gathered round him, and then exclaimed, "Daisy! Is that really you, dear Daisy Deer?" Then looking at the others who were looking down at him and at Daisy Deer, Drip said, "It's Daisy, my old dear friend, Daisy Deer."

Then Drip, to the surprise of the others, scrambled to his feet and then flew up to Daisy Deer, coming to rest on Daisy Deer's snout, giving her a cuddle as only a water gargoyle knows how.

Plop and Plip looked at Drop in surprise, who said, "Well, don't look at me. I'm just as lost as you two are."

On hearing Drop's voice, Daisy Deer said to Drip, "I think these friends of yours deserve an explanation, Drip. But first, I think you should introduce us all."

"You are right, Daisy," said Drip, looking up at Daisy from where he laid on Daisy's snout. "I will do that now."

Drip took off from Daisy's snout. Then once back on the ground, he gathered the others around him and then started to introduce everyone to Daisy Deer, as well as to tell Daisy Deer the names of Drop, Plip and Plop whilst pointing to each one in turn.

"Hello everyone," said Daisy Deer, looking at the water gargoyles who were now seated on the ground. "It's lovely to meet you all."

"Hi, Daisy Deer," said Plip, with a wave and a smile.

"Hello, Daisy Deer," chorused Drop and Plop together, with a little wave as well.

"Daisy Deer," said Plip, who was by now feeling a lot calmer about things. "Would it be possible for you to tell us how you and Drip met, please?"

"I would be delighted to tell you," replied Daisy Deer with a smile as she saw Drip going red with embarrassment. "But first, let me introduce you to my little baby, called Dusty Doe." The baby was peeking from behind Daisy Deer.

Now it is here that I need your help, dear reader, but first, you will need a pencil because every time you see a line, like this, _______, you need to write down either BOY or GIRL on top of the line.

Are you ready? Off we go then.

"Aww, isn't Dusty Doe sweet," said Plip, with Plop nodding in agreement. "Is Dusty a _______ or a _______?

"Dusty Doe is my sweet little _______," replied Daisy Deer, looking at Dusty Doe who was falling asleep, "who was only born yesterday, which is why I'm here."

"I'm glad you are here, Daisy Deer," said Drip, looking at Plip with a smile. "Otherwise, Plip might have been in serious danger."

"Oh, hush now, Drip," said Daisy Deer with a chuckle. "You should know by now that not one creature would hurt you water gargoyles. After all, we all know how you look after us all."

"I'm sorry to be rude, Daisy Deer," said Drop, who was getting impatient. "But would it be possible for you to tell us now how you met my brother please?"

"Of course I can, Drop," replied Daisy Deer with a smile. "I remember it so well because I've never forgotten that cold wet windy night when I got myself trapped in some sort of netting that is used on the big round bales that the farmers leave in the field to dry out, before taking them to the farm. I struggled and struggled until I laid down with exhaustion. Then I cried out, until I couldn't cry out any more, but then, just before I'd given up all hope,

a figure appeared, flying towards me."
"I was out that night because I couldn't sleep," said Drip, taking over from Daisy Deer. "The rain was pouring down and the wind was howling through the forest, yet, for reasons I can't even begin to explain, I sensed that someone was in danger, so I went looking."
"And I'm so glad you did, dear Drip," said Daisy Deer, looking at Drip softly. "If you hadn't had come to my rescue that night, I probably wouldn't be here today with my dear little _______, Dusty Doe."
"So what happened next, Drip?" asked Drop, looking at his brother in a new light.
"Upon arriving next to Daisy Deer," replied Drip, "I could see she had got her hooves trapped in the baling wire. So after calming her down, I set to work in untangling her hooves until she was finally free."
"I never saw Drip again after that night," said Daisy Deer sadly. "But I swore to myself that if I ever come across another like Drip, I will look after them, come what may."
Silence descended upon that little forest glade as everyone looked at Drip and Daisy Deer, as well as take in the story they had just been told. Whilst they were sitting in silence, they heard a bellowing noise, followed by three coughs.
Daisy Deer raised her head and with her ears pricked, she listened, whilst the water gargoyles watched, until she heard the noise again. Then she said, "I'm sorry to say, my dears, but it is time for me to go now, as that is the father of my little _______, Dusty Doe, calling for us."
"Will we see you again?" asked Drip sadly as Daisy Deer and Dusty Doe got to their feet.

"Of course you will, Drip," replied Daisy Deer, bending down to nuzzle Drip.
"That, I will promise you."
And so, we now say goodbye to Daisy Deer and her little _______, Dusty doe, as they leave the forest glade to re-join the little _______ father who is still calling for them.
All of the water gargoyles waved after Daisy Deer and Dusty Doe as they disappeared into the forest, then Drop said, putting his arm around Drip's shoulder, "You will see her again, Drip. I'm sure of it." Then turning to the others, he said, "Come on, it is time for us to get back now."
With a little run and a jump, the four water gargoyles took off into the air, leaving behind the little forest glade, and flew back towards the lake, in silence at first, and then, like always, they all started having fun again. On arriving at the lake, the four water gargoyles decided to fly down towards the lake surface as fast as they can. To see who could leave a water trail behind them, like you would see behind a boat on a river.
For the rest of the day, the water gargoyles played together, playing hide and seek, like you would do with your friends, until finally evening came and the light of the day began to fade.
Drip, Drop, Plip and Plop sat on the grass near the lake's embankment, leaning against the tree, watching the sun slowly disappear, when Plip said, "I had such a wonderful time today"—not really caring if anyone was listening—"that I don't want the time we're having together to end. But I guess we have to go home now."
"I agree with you, Plip," said Plop, with Drip and Drop

nodding in agreement. "But like all good things in life, it has to end at some point, I suppose."
"Oh, I really don't want to go home, though," said Plip, starting to feel annoyed about the whole situation.
"It doesn't have to end if you don't want it to," said Drip with a smile and a chuckle. "As I have an idea but it really depends on how everyone feels about it."
"Well, tell us then, Drip," said Plip, looking at Drip with excitement in her eyes.
"Yes, Drip, tell us what you are thinking," said Plop, grabbing hold of Plip's hand as she was getting excited.
"Why don't we all go and sleep in the nest tonight?" said Drip, laughing at Plip. "That way, we will all still be together in the morning."
"Oh, I don't know about that," said Plop, who couldn't make up her mind at that moment whether she was brave enough or not.
"Actually," said Drop, who suddenly had a thought. "I think it's a really good idea when you think about it."
"Please explain, Drop," said Plop, who had now decided she was brave enough and secretly thought it was a good idea to sleep in the nest after all.
"If we stayed in the nest tonight, we should also hear anything coming in the night and be able to see what is going on. After all, four pair of ears are better than two," said Drop, feeling quite pleased with himself.
"That's a very good point there, Drop," said Plop, looking at Drop with pride.
"Yes it is, isn't it?" said Drip, who was feeling annoyed with himself for not thinking of it instead.
"Well, come on then, you three," said Plip, whose

excitement was finally getting the better of her.
So off they flew up among the trees, until they eventually found the nest that Drip and Drop had spent the previous night in, and then, taking a leaf each from the branch above, they settled down to sleep, under the shining stars. After spending a few days and nights together, Plop and Drop started to become fonder of each other, much to the amusement of Drip and Plip, until one early morning, they were woken to a crashing and grunting noise from down below.
"What was that?" exclaimed Plip, who, like the others, had been woken with fright.
"I don't know, Plip," replied Drip, putting his arm around Plip to give her some reassurance.
"I will go and have a look," said Drop bravely. "You three wait here in the nest until I come back."
"Please be careful, Drop," said Plop as Drop climbed out of the nest. "I don't want to lose you, now that I've found you."
Drop crawled along the branch to get a better look at what the noise was, and to his horror, he saw a two legs, and to make it even worse, the two legs was a fisherman.
"What is it, Drop?" asked Drip as Drop came back after a few minutes and re-joined the others back in the nest.
"It's two legs," replied Drop, looking a little bit pale. "And to make things worse, he is a fisherman!"
"What is a fisherman doing here?" asked Plop, looking puzzled.
"He is here to catch the fish, Plop," said Drop, looking at Plop with sadness. "To take away to eat."
"Oh no," gasped Plop, covering her mouth to stop

herself from crying out. "We need to watch and see where this fisherman goes."
"First of all," said Drop calmly whilst thinking hard. "We need to warn everyone, and I think I might have a plan."
"What are you thinking, Drop?" asked Drip, looking hard at his brother. "Tell us what you want us to do."
"This is what I'm thinking," replied Drop, as he then started to explain. "Drip, I want you to take the two girls back to the lake. Don't leave them until they are safely in the water. Then come back to me. In the meantime, Plop, I want you to go and warn everyone around the lake. And you, Plip, could you go straight to the palace and warn the king and queen and tell them what we are doing, so that they are aware of the plan?"
"No problem," said Drip, signalling to Plip and Plop to follow. "We will go and do that now. See you soon."
"Just a minute," said Plop, whilst looking at Drop. "What are you going to do whilst we are gone, Drop?"
"I'm going to follow the fisherman, using the branches of the trees," said Drop with a smile. "Then, when he has settled down, I will come and join you."
"Oh my goodness," said Plop, not liking the idea of Drop being on his own. "Be careful, will you?" And then, to Drop's surprise, Plop gave him a kiss, before turning to follow Drip and Plip.
Drop watched the others disappear from sight before turning to fly from branch to branch whilst keeping a close eye on the fisherman, not that he really needed to, as the fisherman was making a lot of noise.
Drip, with Plip and Plop, arrived at the lake where

he stood and watched as Plip and Plop silently slid into the water, and then after they had gone, Drip turned and flew back up into the trees to join Drop in following the fisherman.

"You OK, Drop?" asked Drip, upon his return to join Drop.

"Yes, I'm fine," replied Drop, feeling a bit uncomfortable all of a sudden.

"OK," said Drip with a chuckle before flying to the next branch.

"Why do you ask?" asked Drop as he flew past Drip to land onto the next branch.

"I noticed you went red when Plop kissed you," replied Drip, flying past Drop to land on a branch in a tree further along, which was above where the fisherman was standing.

"Drip, shut up about it before you start," said Drop, smiling to himself, as he flew to join Drip on the branch above the fisherman.

"You like Plop, don't you, Drop"? asked Drip, deciding he wasn't going to let Drop off that easy, as they both watched the fisherman move further on along the lake.

"I don't know, Drip," replied Drop, who for some reasons felt like he had butterflies in his belly, "I admit that I do like Plop a lot, especially since we have gotten to know each other over the last few days."

"Now that wasn't too hard to admit, was it?" asked Drip, looking at Drop's face and smiling as it started to go red with embarrassment.

"I don't know," replied Drop, smiling, and then nodding towards the disappearing figure. "But we better get going before the fisherman disappears."

The two brothers took off from where they were standing to carry on following the fisherman, until finally they saw him unfold a chair and begin to settle down whilst putting together his equipment. Satisfied that the fisherman wasn't going to move, Drip and Drop flew back the way they came, and then, when they knew they were out of sight, they slid into the lake.

After entering the lake, the two brothers swam back towards the fisherman. On their way, they saw Mr Salmon, who went and informed Plip and Plop that Drip and Drop were back in the lake, after having everything explained to him.

As Drip and Drop got nearer to the fisherman, they saw a hook in the water tied to a fishing line, and above that, part way in and out of the lake surface, was a round red float.

"Be careful, Drip," warned Drop as he noticed Drip swimming closer to the hook.

"I will, don't worry," said Drip, as he had noticed something on the fishing line.

As Drip swam closer, he noticed that the fishing line had round metal things clamped to it above the hook. Must be weights to keep the fishing line steady, Drip thought to himself whilst being careful to avoid the hook.

Whilst Drip was looking, a strong wind blew above the lake that also caused a strong currant below, so strong in fact that it moved Drip and the fishing line closer together, which caused Drip to grab hold of the line.

By doing this, Drip thought, it would keep him safe from the hook but what he didn't realise was that when he grabbed hold of it, the float above him

sunk downwards.

The fisherman, sitting on the embankment, saw the float sink downwards and grabbed hold of his fishing rod. He then pulled the fishing rod upwards and towards him, thinking he had caught a fish.

"NOOO," screamed Drop loudly, filled with fright as he saw the hook shoot upwards, taking poor Drip with it.

Drop's screams brought Plip and Plop rushing over, as they were nearby anyway and since Mr Salmon had already seen and told them where they could find Drip and Drop.

"What happened?" asked Plop, taking Drop's grieve-stricken face gently into her hands. "Tell me everything, Drop. Don't leave anything out," Plop then said calmly.

Drop then proceeded to explain what had happened, to Plip and Plop, whilst fighting back the tears and anger of what had happened to poor Drip.

"Oh no, poor Drip," said Plip, looking at Drop with eyes filled with tears. "We need to go and find him."

"I'm going after him," said Drop, filling up with anger. "And I'm not letting anyone, including that fisherman, from stopping me," Drop then said to Plop as Plop tried to stop him.

"STOP RIGHT THERE," said the king loudly and sternly as he came closer to Drop, Plop and Plip, followed closely behind by ten of the palace guards.

"But, sir, my brother..." said Drop angrily whilst pointing in the direction Drip went.

"I know Drop, I know," said the king more calmly as he swam over to Drop. "This is the time for wise thinking," the king then said, taking hold of Drop's arms. "But first you need to calm down, laddie, because being angry won't solve anything, apart from making things worse. And when the queen gets here, and you can be assured she will as she is on her way, we will sort this out together. In the meantime, Plip and Plop can go and start looking for him."

"Er, sir..." said Plop to the king, feeling frightened all of a sudden, "Me and Plip haven't been out of the lake before, without Drip and Drop."

"Then it is about time you both learnt," said the king sternly, releasing Drop's arms as he turned to face Plop. "Drip needs you both, now more than ever before."

"Right, OK then," said Plop, not really knowing how to respond to the king. "Come on, Plip, the sooner we go, the sooner we can get back."

But before they could leave, the king said, "Go to the edge and then climb up the embankment. Once you have made sure you are not in any danger, fly up into the trees, using them to keep yourselves hidden from the fisherman."

"Will do," said Plop, who was now feeling more confident after listening to the king's advice.

Plip and Plop swam to the edge of the lake and then slowly raised their heads above the water, always looking around for the fisherman. Once they saw there was no danger, they climbed up the embankment.

When they reached the top, they then crawled through the grass, until they were among the trees, and it was here, they took to the air, not realising the two palace guards were sent to watch over them.

Whilst waiting, the king, with Drop and the rest of the guards, went into the reeds that grew on the bottom of the lake, to keep out of sight, and sat down in silence as they waited for Plip and Plop to return.

After an hour was gone by, Plip and Plop reappeared into the lake and then swam over to Drop, who had appeared from among the reeds upon seeing them, still not seeing the two guards following them.

"We looked everywhere, Drop," said Plop sadly. But Drop already knew before Plop said anything, as he could see the look on their faces that told him everything he needed to know.

"We flew up into the trees, as well as crawled as close as we dared to the fisherman," said Plip, who was now in tears, as was Plop. "But we still couldn't find him. I'm so sorry, Drop."

Drop took hold of Plip and Plop, holding them both close to him as they both cried whilst fighting back his own tears, as he looked up towards the sun from the bottom of the lake.

Through all of this, no one had noticed the queen had arrived, with more guards, and was standing behind a rock, listening to the cries and sensing Drop's strength failing him.

She then summoned a guard and informed him to tell the king of her arrival. Once the guard has left, the queen called her magic to her, and then, with the guards following, she swam over to Drop, Plip and Plop.

As the queen swam closer, she started to grow bigger and bigger, as well as her wings, until she reached the three water gargoyles, and then, very

gently, she folded her wings around them.
"Hello, my dears," said the queen softly. Then she held her hand up to stop Plop from speaking. "It is alright. I heard everything that you and Plip have said to Drop. Now, I must ask you all to be silent for just a moment."
As they stood there in silence, they noticed the queen's eyes turn into a golden glow as she concentrated on finding Drip, and then the queen said, whispering her words, "I can see him, and he is safe and sound. Yet he is not alone, he is with one who is his dear friend, whom he saw earlier, in a clearing in the forest."
Then with a gasp, the queen came back to herself, and as she did so, the golden glow in her eyes disappeared. She then asked whilst putting her wings away, "Do you know where he is?"
"He is with Daisy Deer," replied Plip with a squeal. "I'm sure of it."
"He must be, Drop," said Plop, looking at Drop with excitement. "It's the only forest clearing we know of."
"It's the only place I can think of too," said Drop, relieved at knowing Drip is alive and well. "But what I don't understand is how he got there."
"You are not going to find out while you are still here," said the queen, laughing and smiling. "Well, go on then. Go and get him, and bring him back to me."
"Damn and blast," said a voice rather crossly from among the reeds. "Every time them water gargoyles take off in a hurry, I'm always the one to suffer for it. And now, I'm stuck in among these blasted reeds."
The queen, seeing what had happened, summoned two of her guards and said, "Be a dear and go help Mr Salmon, please. He seems to be tangled up in

the reeds."

Drip flew through the air as he was still gripping tightly to the fishing line, until he let go. Drip tried to open his wings, but because he was spinning in the air, he couldn't manage it.

Poor Drip ended up crashing into a tree, further behind the fisherman, and then fell to the ground where he laid, battered and bruised. As he lay there, a shadow came over him.

"It's OK, Drip. I've got you now," said a gentle voice.

"Daisy Deer," groaned Drip, weakly and unable to move. "Is it really you or am I imagining things?"

"It's me, dear Drip," replied Daisy Deer quietly. "Now be quiet, as the fisherman is still close by. And whatever you do, don't struggle."

"OK," said Drip, finally succumbing to the darkness.

Daisy Deer bent down and took Drip into her mouth, then very quietly, she moved away from the fisherman, glancing back at regular intervals, until she was sure they were safe.

Then, with a leap forward, Daisy Deer took to her hooves and ran as fast as she could into the forest. As she ran, she wondered where to take Drip, finally deciding on going back to the little forest glade.

It was there that Drop, with Plip and Plop, found Drip, lying on the ground, in between Daisy Deer's front legs, with Daisy Deer watching him like a mother watches over her child.

"Drip, are you OK?" asked Plip softly, kneeling next to Drip.

"I'm OK, my love," replied Drip, still in a daze, taking hold of Plip's hand.

"How did you end up back here?" asked Drop as he took hold of Drip and cuddled him.

"Daisy Deer found me and brought me here," replied Drip, wincing in pain from being cuddled too tightly by Drop.
"He seems to be fine," said Daisy Deer softly. "But I'm afraid he won't be going anywhere, not without any help, as he is bruised all over.
"Don't worry, Daisy Deer. We will take care of him now," said Plop, looking up at Daisy Deer. "And thank you so much for rescuing him."
"You are very welcome, dear Plop," said Daisy Deer, looking down at Drip. "But now I must go, as I've been gone from my little _______, Dusty Doe, for far too long now."
Daisy Deer carefully got to her feet, so as not to cause Drip, or anyone else, any injuries, and then started to walk away but not before turning round and saying, "I will be close by as much as I can, until I see Drip is well again. So for now, I will say goodbye."
After saying their goodbyes and sending their thanks to Daisy Deer, Drop turned to Plip and said, "Let me take him now, Plip." And then proceeded to lift Drip up into his arms.
"Are you going to manage him, Drop?" asked Plop, helping Drop get to his feet.
"I will be fine," replied Drop. Then turning to Plip, he said, "Can you fly ahead and warn the king and queen we're on our way back, please."
"No, I'm sorry Drop," said Plip kindly whilst still looking at Drip. "I want to stay with Drip if you don't mind."
"I will go, Drop," said Plop, before Drop could say anything. "I would be the same as Plip if it was you instead of Drip."

Drop then opened his wings, and with a smile at Drip, he took off into the air, with Plip flying close by, whilst Plop flew off ahead to warn the king and queen of their arrival, as well as to tell them how Drip is.

Upon arriving at the lake, Plip slipped into the water and went on to tell the king and queen that Drop was waiting with Drip amongst the trees, as he didn't want to risk the fisherman seeing them.

On hearing this, the queen sent all the guards out of the lake to distract the fisherman, and all the fisherman saw was bright silver light, flashing backwards and forwards, of the palace guards.

Whilst the fisherman was temporarily blinded by the bright silver light, Drop took off again until he was above the lake, and then, very slowly, he lowered himself to the lake surface until the very last moment.

On seeing Drop appear in the lake, still holding Drip, the queen, with the king, Plip and Plop, came over to him as Drop laid Drip onto the floor. In the meantime, the guards reappeared to stand around them.

The queen bent over Drip and started to grow in size, again. As she did so, she took Drip into her arms, then standing up, she unfolded her wings and wrapped them around Drip.

The king put his hands on Drop's shoulder and beckoned him and the rest of the water gargoyles to move back a little bit, and then he said to Drop, patting Drop's shoulder, "Drip will be alright now."

As the queen stood still, whilst holding Drip, there was a sudden flash of gold. So sudden, in fact, that the entire lake surface flashed gold, making the fisherman above jump back in fright, sending him backwards over his chair.

After the sudden flash, the queen laid Drip gently on the ground, at the bottom off the lake, whilst shrinking back down to her normal size.

"Wake up, Drip," said Plip, who had rushed to kneel by Drip's side. "It's me, Plip."

"Drip," said Drop, shaking Drip's shoulder gently. "Come on, wake up!"

But Drip wasn't waking up at all.

"Kiss him, Plip," said the king, with a twinkle in his eye.

"Pardon," said Plip, looking at the king in surprise.

"Trust me, my dear," said the king, with a chuckle.

"Well, OK then," said Plip, who secretly wanted to kiss Drip anyway.

Plip then bent her head forward towards Drip's and then gently kissed him on the lips. Whilst this was going on, Drip's arms came up and around Plip's waist, making Plip jump back in surprise.

"Can you do that again, please?" said Drip to Plip, making her smile.

Drop then came forward and took his brother into his arms, holding him tight, and then said, as Drip hugged him back, "You know something, Drip, you really can be a prize drip sometimes."

It made everyone laugh, including Drip, who was wincing from the pain caused by his bruises.

"How did you know that a kiss would bring Drip back round, your majesty?" asked Plop, out of curiosity.

"Well, I didn't," replied the king with a mischievous look in his eye. "But it works on the queen every morning, so I thought it might work on Drip too."

The king's words made everyone smile, but when the queen called the king a soppy old man, this

caused everyone to start laughing, making poor Drip wince in pain again.
"Now it is time for us to see if we can use the fisherman to our advantage," said the queen, to everyone's surprise.
"What do you mean, my dear?" asked the king, knowing when trouble is coming.
"We are going to get rid of those horrible looking items," replied the queen, looking at the items with disgust. "And we are going to get the fisherman to remove them."
I knew it, thought the king, looking skywards.
"What do you want us to do, your majesty?" asked Drip eagerly.
"You are not going to do anything, Drip," said Plip sternly. "You are in too much pain to do anything but rest."
"I agree with Plip, I'm afraid, Drip," said the queen to Drip, with the king nodding in agreement. "Which is why Plip is going to take you home and put you to bed."
"OK, your majesty," said Drip sulkily.
Then Plip, with Drop's help, got Drip to his feet and then took him home, but not before Drop said, "I will be home as soon as I can, Drip."
"OK, Drop, I will see you soon," said Drip as he hobbled off, with Plip helping him, as the others watched, until they disappeared from sight.
"Drop," said the queen, making sure she had Drop's attention. "Can you go to the surface and see if the fisherman is still there, please?"
"No problem, your majesty," said Drop, who then swam to the surface of the lake to have a look. On arriving back, Drop reported that the fisherman

was still there and was fiddling with his fishing line.
"I see," said the queen, looking at the guards and beckoning one over. "We will have to be quick then."
"What do you want us to do, your majesty?" asked Plop, not really knowing where she stood in the matter.
"You, Plop," said the queen, looking at Plop, "will stay here by mine and the king's side."
Then turning to the guard, the queen said, "Take the men nearer to the fisherman, and when he throws the hook, I want all of you to take flight and distract him like before." Then turning to Drop, she said, "I want you to go to the surface again and keep watch. As soon as you see the guards fly from the lake, you must come straight back to me."
"What will you do, your majesty?" asked Drop curiously.
"Don't worry about me," replied the queen sternly. "Just do as I asked of you. Now, can everyone get into position and be ready to move."
Drop and the guards left their majesties, with Plop standing by them, to go and get into position, but as soon as they arrived, the fisherman flicked his rod, sending the hook sailing into the lake.
As soon as he sat down in his chair, the guards flew out of the lake, startling the fisherman so much, he went head over heels, taking the chair with him. Meanwhile, as luck would have it, the hook landed near the items.
Drop, on seeing the guards move, swam back to their majesties and Plop, as fast as he could, but the queen was already moving, as she had seen the hook appear in the lake.
The queen swam towards the hook, with Plop by

her side, growing bigger as she got closer to hook. Then when she was big enough, she grabbed hold of the hook and pulled.

The queen, with Plop's help, pulled the hook towards the items, then she fed the hook through everything she could, then she tied the hook off. Whilst this was happening, the king swam to the surface to keep watch.

Once everything was done to the queen's satisfaction, she called her guards back to her. Then, with everyone following, she led them all into the reeds, to hide, to listen and watch to see what happens next.

The fisherman got back to his feet, muttering to himself, then bent down to retrieve his fishing rod, but when he tried to reel the fishing line back in, he found that he couldn't do that.

"Well, what a strange day this has been," said the fisherman to himself. "Strange sparkling silver objects and now, my blasted line is tangled up with something."

The fisherman then pulled on some waterproofs, then proceeded to walk into the lake, causing the silt on the bottom to swirl around, making it difficult for the water gargoyles to see what was happening.

As he came closer, he stumbled upon the items, then with his hands, he reached in to grab hold of one of the items and lifted it to the surface. "Now what disgusting person would throw a shopping trolley and a bicycle into a lake. They should be ashamed of themselves," he said as he retrieved the other item.

The water gargoyles heard all this as they went further back into the reeds and started to smile

with delight in seeing the items disappear from the lake, then the king turned to Drop and Plop, and said, "At last, we know now what they are."
"Yes, we do," said the queen. Then turning to one of the guards, she said, "Can you go and have a look and see if the fisherman is gone?"
With a nod, the guard left to see if the fisherman had gone, only to find him sitting back in his chair, trying to untangle the fishing line. So the guard reported this to the queen upon his return.
"Now it is time for all to return to the safety of our homes," said the queen, with a smile. "But quietly, please, as we don't want to be seen by the fisherman."
"I'm pleased you said that, your majesty," said Drop, looking at the queen with a smile, "as I'm rather anxious to go to Drip."
"And you should be, my dear," said the queen, with a smile. "But I'm expecting regular reports on how Drip is doing, mind."
"Me and Plip will keep you informed," said Plop to the queen and taking Drop's hand in hers. "But before we go, what is going to happen to the fisherman"?
"Don't you worry about him, my dear," said the queen, with a chuckle. "My guards, with the others, will keep an eye on him. And I will make sure you are informed if anything happens."
After everyone had said their goodbyes, Drop and Plop, holding hands, slowly but surely, swam back to the island, then entered the tunnel that led to the homes of the water gargoyles.
"Hello, you two," Drop called out, as he and Plop entered the home of Drip and Drop. "Where are you both"?

"We're in Drip's bedroom," replied Plip, pleased to see Drop and Plop.
"Hello, you pair," said Drip, lying in bed. "What's been happening?"
"Oh yes, please tell us," said Plip excitedly. "Don't leave anything out."
"Oh my, what a story to tell," replied Drop, with a smile. Then with Plop's help, he told Drip and Plip what had happened, as well as telling them what the items were called and that they were now gone from the lake.
"Oh that is good to hear," said Plip happily. "Isn't it, Drip?"
"Yes, it is," replied Drip, smiling. "I want to get up now though."
"Absolutely not," said Plip sternly. "You are staying in bed."
"But I'm bored, Plip," said Drip, knowing full well he was not going to win this argument, but he was going to give it a good go anyway.
"Bored!" exclaimed Plip, even more sternly. "How can you possibly be bored when you have only been in bed ten minutes?"
"Yes, but I–" said Drip, who was then interrupted by Plip.
"I'm not discussing it, Drip," said Plip, getting cross. "You will stay where you are and you WILL do what you are told."
Chuckling to himself, Drop gently took hold of Plop's arm, then with Plop beside him, they moved into the hallway, out of earshot of Plip and Drip arguing, then he said, "You can tell he is on the mend, can't you"?
"Yes, you can," replied Plop, laughing. "He is also

going to learn that Plip won't let him have his way all the time either."

"Oh I can see that for myself," said Drop with a chuckle. Then he continued saying, "Thank you, Plop, for everything you have done to help me. I don't know what I would have done without you by my side."

"You are welcome, my dear," said Plop, then taking Drop's face into her hands, Plop kissed him lightly on the lips.

"Wow," said Drop afterwards. "I don't know what to say or do now."

"You will, in time," said Plop with a smile. Then turning back to Drip's bedroom, Plop called to Plip to say it was time to go home.

After Plip and Plop left, Drop went back in to Drip's bedroom, only to find Drip sitting up in bed.

"How you feeling, Drip"? asked Drop, moving to sit on the bed.

"I'm a lot better," replied Drip, looking at his brother. "How about you?"

"I'm fine," replied Drop, nodding and looking towards the hallway.

"Missing Plop, are you"? said Drip airily.

"I don't know what you are talking about," replied Drop sharply but without much conviction.

"Drop," said Drip kindly. "It will be OK, you know. Just think of it as a life's adventure."

"But it is scary," said Drop, who was feeling a bit worried.

"Yes," said Drip, laughing at Drop. "But it is nice as well."

"Yes," said Drop, agreeing with Drip. Then Drop smiled and said, "You are right, Drip. It is nice to fall in love."

Over the next few days, Plip and Plop came round to help Drop, with Drip, and to report to the king and queen on Drip's progress, until one warm evening, Drip and Plip, with Drop and Plop, burst forth from the lake to fly up among the canopy of the trees.
"Oh it's so good to be out in the fresh air again," said Drip, taking deep breaths. "And I can see that the fisherman and the items have gone as well."
"Yes, and it's lovely to feel the breeze on my face again," said Plip, stretching whilst in mid-air.
"Why don't we all stay in the nest tonight"? asked Plop. Then turning to Drop, Plop asked, "What do you think, Drop?"
"That sounds lovely, my love," replied Drop to Plop. Then taking Plop's hand, he said, "Come on, let's go."
With that, Drop and Plop flew among the trees, looking for the nest, followed closely behind by Drip and Plip, until they found the nest. Then they all settled down, with a big leaf each to cover two water gargoyles.
And there they stayed, watching the sun go down and the stars appear as the sky turned dark with the arrival of night time, and it is there we will leave our friends, the water gargoyles, to sleep.
So if ever you find yourself beside a lake, with trees around it, look carefully around you, as you may just see a silver sparkle or a golden glow, and if you do, you will know you have found the home of Drip and Drop.

The End